AS WAY LEADS ONTO WAY

Happy reading //

Michael Zigie

AS WAY LEADS ONTO WAY

MICHAEL LAJOIE

Reddington Press

To those who weathered the way it was—
and held out hope for the way it would be.

Also by Michael Lajoie

The Summit by the Sea

Contents

I	1
II	7
III	13
IV	17
V	24
VI	32
VII	36
VIII	41
IX	48
X	55
XI	59

"And both that morning equally lay
In leaves no step had trodden black.
Oh, I kept the first for another day!
Yet knowing how way leads onto way,
I doubted if I should ever come back..."

— *Robert Frost, "The Road Not Taken"*

WINTER 1932

BURLINGTON, VERMONT

U.S.A.

I

Silas leaned back in his chair, considering the contents of his cup. The coffee within was hot and black and bitter. It stained the bright enamelware with rings of liver spot brown, sharply declaring its dwindling existence. He brought the half-empty cup to his lips but refrained from drinking. The past three sips had burned going down, but they had brought him little warmth. He sighed, glancing out the café's great glass window. A sluggish crowd of people was struggling through the slush of the street, their heads lowered against the wind.

He shivered sympathetically. Winter's chill was cruel and creeping. The clouds were constant and the sun was scarcely seen. Life in this lakeside city was cold and gray.

It was not a traditional city by any means—not at all like the ones portrayed in the moving pictures. There were no skyscrapers, no bridges, and no booming stock exchange. All of that could be found in New York, hundreds of miles south, where the exchange had since died and winter was certainly the coldest. Burlington, in the north, was very much its own brand—an old, intellectual heap of brick houses and greenish copper cupolas. The university spire was its tallest structure, and the towering chapel on campus was its second. It was purely a city because of the number of people that lived there—around twenty thousand stone-faced New Englanders and suit-clad university men. Silas was one of them. He had been for three years.

He surveyed the café with another sigh. It was quiet and dim, and only one other table was occupied. The man, like him, was sitting on his own. He had thick, furrowed eyebrows and a stern-looking mustache. His eyes were sharp and scrutinizing, and his slate-colored suit was impeccably pressed and pleated. Today's newspaper was spread out in front of him, but he paid it no mind. He was scowling down at his bowl of oatmeal, which sat untouched beneath his molten gaze.

Silas watched the waiter approach the table and ask, good-naturedly, if the scowling man was enjoying his breakfast.

"No," the scowling man grumbled. "I'm not."

The waiter glanced at the oatmeal's undisturbed surface. "Very sorry to hear that, sir," he said. "Is there something wrong with the dish?"

The scowling man seized his spoon from the table and stabbed it into the bowl. He stirred the oatmeal crossly, glowering at the rising curls of steam. "Just how do you expect me to eat this?" he demanded.

"What's wrong with it?" the waiter asked. "Is it insufficiently seasoned? I'll fetch you some nutmeg, sir—some cinnamon, too."

"This has nothing to do with the seasoning," the scowling man snapped. "Look at the steam, will you? These oats are too damned hot!"

"Terribly sorry, sir," the waiter said. "Let me bring you some ice."

"I don't want ice," the scowling man said sharply. "That'll just water it down." He threw his hands up at the bowl. "What's the matter with you, serving food that's too hot to eat? Don't you have any sense at all?"

"Many people complain the food is too cold," the waiter explained. "We serve it hot to keep them happy."

"Is that so?" The man's scowl was seared into the lines of his face. "Do I look happy right now?"

The waiter looked away temporarily, clearing his throat. "Could I offer you something else off the menu? There are many fine options for breakfast."

"If they're served as hot as the oatmeal," the scowling man said, "then absolutely not." His face was quickly turning a dark shade of red. "I ordered oats because I wanted oats—not because I wanted this intolerable slop!"

"If it's not too bold of me, sir," the waiter said. "Couldn't you just wait for your oats to cool?"

"I didn't come here to wait. I came here to eat."

"Of course, sir. Your oats should be cool in no time at all."

The scowling man slammed his fist on the table and across the room, Silas jumped. "I don't have time to wait!" he roared. "I'm far too busy a man for this sort of nonsense!"

The waiter flinched. "What would you like me to do about this?"

The scowling man sat fuming before his oatmeal, then shoved the bowl away. "Bring me the bill."

The waiter withdrew the bill from his apron and placed it on the table.

The scowling man glared at it and crossed his arms. "I have a good mind not to pay this at all," he said.

"You must pay it, sir. It's the law."

"I have a good mind not to."

The waiter remained by the table. "Please, sir. I ask that you pay the bill."

Still very red in the face, the scowling man reached into his suit jacket and pulled out the money. He tossed it onto the table, grabbed his newspaper, and jammed his hat onto his head. "Absolutely no time for this," he muttered, then stormed out of the café into the cold.

Silas sipped his coffee, which had since cooled, and watched the scowling man leave. The waiter shook his head at the door and began clearing the table. He collected the scowling man's money, folded it over the bill, and then disappeared into the kitchen with the uneaten bowl of oatmeal. When he returned, he stopped at Silas's table.

"At your convenience, sir," he said, setting the bill next to the coffee cup. He lingered for a second, his face taut with hesitation. "And how was everything this morning?"

Silas smiled. "Excellent," he said. "The oatmeal was terrific."

"Very good," the waiter said, sounding significantly relieved. "That's what you always have, isn't it? Oatmeal, a coffee, and wheat toast?"

"That's right."

"Yes," the waiter said. "I've seen you in here before. The university man with the book..." He squinted, trying to remember. "What was the name of it again? You told me once. The story about the thorough man who leaves the city to live by a pond."

"*Walden*—by Henry David Thoreau."

"That's the one."

"It's a great book."

"Have you finished it yet?"

"I have."

"How did you like it?"

"I loved it."

"Would you recommend it?"

"Definitely," Silas said. "Although I'll warn you: it'll make you want to pack up your life and leave everything behind."

The waiter chuckled. "That sounds particularly good right now. It's been quite a morning."

"I heard," Silas said. "Hot oatmeal—what a ridiculous thing to get so upset about."

"It couldn't have just been the oatmeal."

"No, you're right. There was probably more."

"What do you think it was?"

"I don't know," Silas said. "I'm sure the state of things had him feeling down."

"They have me feeling down," the waiter said.

"Yeah. Me, too."

They stared out the great glass window in silence. There was frost glistening along the edges of the pane.

Silas drained the rest of his coffee. "The world is cold," he said. That was the conclusion he always reached.

"It is," the waiter agreed. "Especially this time of year. Sometimes it feels like winter will never end."

"I'm not so sure that it ever really does," Silas said. He stared down at the empty coffee cup.

"I can bring you some more," the waiter offered.

"That's all right."

"Are you sure?"

"Yeah. I'll be leaving soon, anyway. I have a train to catch at ten." Silas checked his watch. It was a quarter past nine.

"I was wondering why you were dressed down," the waiter said, surveying his lumberjack appearance. "No class today?"

"Not today." He hesitated. "Well, there is, but I can't afford to miss the train. I'm spending the weekend in Freedman's Notch."

"That's a valley, isn't it?"

"Yes, in the mountains across the lake."

"Is there an inn there?"

"I believe so—hopefully."

The waiter gave him a funny smile. "You don't know?"

Silas shrugged. "I'll find out."

"Freedman's Notch..." The waiter knitted his brow. "I can't say I know much about it. Enjoy yourself, all the same."

Silas nodded. "I will. I've been needing some time away."

"We all have," the waiter said. He paused. "Any idea of how cold it'll be?"

"Cold—but it can't be much colder there than it is here."

"Well, good luck to you."

"Thanks." Silas looked down, remembering the bill by the coffee cup. He retrieved some money from the inner pocket of his overcoat, shivering at the thick wad of dollars that lay tucked against his heart. He laid it out on the table, tipped the waiter well, and then rose from his seat.

The waiter smiled. "Always a pleasure, sir."

"Always."

"Stay warm."

Silas pulled his rucksack up from beneath the table. The pair of snowshoes strapped to either side of it clacked as he hoisted it onto his back. "I'll do my best," he said.

He savored the last of the café's warmth, then went out onto the street.

II

A crowd of scowling people streamed around him as he buttoned up his overcoat. The waiter was right—he was dressed down. It felt strange to think that his gray university suit and polished black dress shoes were now neatly packed away in his dormitory closet. He had swapped them out for something warmer—a thick plaid flannel and a sturdy pair of leather hiking boots. He seldom wore them around campus, but this weekend, he was leaving the university behind. He was headed for the happiness that lingered beyond the lake.

Lake Champlain was only a mile down the hill from the university, and Silas routinely sought peace by its shores. The view from the docks faced west, and it never failed to soothe his buzzing mind. He liked to watch the sun glide over the frozen surface of the water and take refuge behind the snow-covered mountains on the other side. It would hover above their hulking flanks, only about as bright as the flame from a tallow candle, and beckoned to him with fleeting urgency. Warmth, it assured him, would be found in the stark evergreen wilderness that lay on the opposite shore.

He had spent many evenings gazing at the mountains from the edge of the waterfront pier, yearning for the escape that he knew they could provide for him. They loomed solemnly in the distance, white and wistful in the dusk. There was an undeniable beauty in their windswept gorges and ice-encrusted summits that he was eager to explore.

Now, finally, he was answering their call. A two-way ticket to Freedman's Notch was tucked in the pocket against his chest, and he beamed at the prospect of the trip ahead of him. It would be nice to get away from it all—from the depression, and from the state of things. The world was resoundingly cold, and hardly anybody was happy anymore. The chill had twisted every face into a smoldering scowl.

He remembered the way it was before the scowls set in, when the world drank to the news from Versailles and spent the next decade celebrating the end of the war. Back then, every cup was full—so full that rich, tannic alcohol sloshed over the rim and down the sides. He had come to the university with wide eyes and an even wider grin, thrilled by Burlington's blaring jazz and boundless delights. The market was booming, spirits were soaring, and the days were warm and bright. The roaring times had Uncle Sam enraptured, and nobody—not even President Hoover—had predicted they would end.

But they did end, with a crash. Stocks plummeted midway through his first semester, and countless banks went under. Not long after, winter descended upon the city. Homes and businesses froze from the inside out, and enrollment stalled at the university. Silas watched it all from his lofty dormitory window, ridden with guilt over the money that kept him sheltered from the cold.

He had weathered the winter for the past three years, weighed down by its frigid toll on those around him. Less than a week ago, as he was walking home from class, he had come across a cowering line of men on the sidewalk.

"Hello," he had said to one of them. "What are you waiting for?"

The man stared down at his feet. There was shame lurking in his sullen eyes. "Food," he mumbled. "Can't you read the sign?"

Silas traced the line to the door of a modest-looking bakery. A glaring white banner was hanging in the window.

HOOVER CAKES, it read. *FREE FOR THE UNEMPLOYED.*

He looked down at his gray university suit, then back at the shamefaced man. "I'm sorry."

"Don't be," the shamefaced man said. He nodded at the banner in the window. "Ever had one?"

"A Hoover Cake? No, I can't say I have. What are they?"

"Nothing special—just biscuits dusted with powdered sugar."

"Are they any good?"

"Not really."

"What do they taste like?"

"Nothing. They're bland and cold."

"Ha," Silas said. "Just like the president."

"To hell with the president," the shamefaced man growled. "He sees us starving and turns the other way. He only cares about the rich. To hell with him."

"To hell with him," Silas agreed. "The world is cold—almost as cold as he is."

The shamefaced man studied him closely. "You really think that?"

Silas nodded. "Of course."

"Hm. All right, then."

"Why do you sound so surprised?"

"I don't know," the shamefaced man said. "It might be the way you carry yourself, or maybe it's the way you're dressed."

"What about it?"

"You look warm," he said. "Comfortable. What reason do you have to hate Hoover? You don't look hungry at all."

"I'm not," Silas admitted. "But it makes no difference. The cold weighs on me just the same."

"I suppose it weighs on a lot of people nowadays," the shamefaced man said. "The city is a cold place to live. I'd escape it, if I could."

"Why can't you?"

"I may not have a job," he said, "but I have a line to wait in. I have a family to feed. The city's their home, even if it doesn't feel like mine. So, I have no choice but to stay."

"I'm sorry," Silas said again.

"Don't be," the shamefaced man said. "For Christ's sake, don't be." He gestured limply to the rest of the cowering line. "We get enough pity. Lord knows we'd be a hell of a lot happier without it."

Silas said nothing, feeling extremely conscious of his gray university suit. The other shamefaced men avoided his solemn gaze.

"Anyway," the shamefaced man continued. "I can't afford to leave the city. Not now. Not while my family needs me." He scratched his unshaven chin. "But what about you?"

"What about me?" Silas said.

"I'm sure you can afford to leave the city. You're young, but you don't look old enough to have a family to feed. Am I wrong?"

"No, you're right. I have a family, but they feed themselves just fine. I live here by myself."

"Then what's stopping you from leaving?"

Silas looked down at the slush on the sidewalk. "The same thing that's stopping you," he said. "I have responsibilities."

"Like what?"

"Tedious things—lectures to attend, books to read, and papers to write. The work never stops."

"Ah," the shamefaced man said. "You're a university man, aren't you?"

"That's right."

"So, you *can* afford to leave the city."

"Yes, I suppose I can."

"Have you?"

"Not since before the crash."

"Three years," the shamefaced man said. "You haven't left the city in three years."

"I know," Silas said, and the cold truth weighed on him. "I could use some time away."

"We all could," the shamefaced man said. "But the difference between you and the rest of us is that you could actually get it. You're a university man. You have money—money that you could use to afford yourself an escape."

"Or," Silas said, "money that I could give to someone else. There are clearly people who need it more than me."

"That sounds a hell of a lot less than genuine."

"I'm sorry. I just wish I could help."

The shamefaced man squinted at his suit. "We don't need your help."

"But you need money, don't you?"

The shamefaced man shook his head. "Use it for yourself. It's yours."

"I have enough," Silas insisted. "Won't you take some of it?"

The shamefaced man hid his hands in his pockets. "No, sir. Not a chance."

"Why not?"

He lowered his voice, along with his embarrassed eyes. "Money is the coldest form of pity," he muttered.

Silas nodded. "I understand."

"Use it for yourself," the shamefaced man repeated. "Use it to buy an escape. It doesn't matter where you go, just as long as it's far away from here. Hop on a train and leave the cold behind."

A gust of wind tore down the street, wailing at the crowds with wicked fury. Silas braced himself against the chill, scouring his mind for warm thoughts. Immediately, he recalled the soothing view from the waterfront pier. The mountains, bone-white in his memory, beckoned to him from across the lake.

"Think about it, at least," the shamefaced man said. "Lord knows I would, if I could afford it."

"I will," Silas said, and not long afterward, he did.

He bought his ticket to Freedman's Notch the following morning.

III

Silas shuffled his way through the crowd, trying to think of the fastest route to the train station. He considered hailing a cab but, in the end, he decided the walk would do him good. There was still ample time before the train arrived, and the station wasn't that far away. He set off down the hill, toward the lake.

Both sides of the street were lined with old, ivy-obscured houses that peered at him from behind their wrought iron gates. Their doors and windows were tightly shut in an effort to keep out the chill, and the frigid air was heavy with the smoke of their blazing fireplaces. Many of the houses' occupants belonged to the bustling crowd, which drove him along like an unremitting current. He lifted his gaze above the flow of people, silently searching for the distant horizon. It was just visible through a gap in the crisscrossing canopy of telephone wires overhead. He caught a glimpse of the blueish outlines of the mountains across the lake and smiled. Very soon, he would be among them.

As Silas lowered his gaze to the crowd, he gradually became aware of an old man sitting at the base of a lamppost on the edge of the street. He was huddled beneath a threadbare blanket, avoiding the condescending glares of the few passersby that cared enough to look at him. He was an uninhabited island amid a swirling sea of people, and Silas had never seen anybody so alone.

He slowed his pace, coming to a halt beside him. "Hello," he said.

"What do you want?" the old man growled. "You're not here to tell me to leave, are you?" He narrowed his sunken eyes. "Because I'm not going anywhere."

"Not at all," Silas said earnestly. "I was just stopping to say hello."

"I can't remember the last time someone did that," the old man said bitterly.

Silas gestured to the lamppost. "Do you mind if I sit?"

The old man nodded and Silas sat. "How are you?" he asked.

"Cold," the old man said, rewrapping himself in his blanket. "Cold and hungry, but still alive." He considered Silas for a moment. "What's your name?"

"Silas. What's yours?"

"Job."

"Good to meet you, Job." Silas offered the old man his hand.

Job stared. "You want to shake my hand?"

Silas nodded. "Why wouldn't I?"

"I'm old, dirty, and homeless," Job said. "Aren't you afraid that'll rub off on you?"

"No," Silas said.

Slowly, Job shook his hand. "Who *are* you?" he said.

"A friend," Silas replied.

They sat in silence, watching the current of people flow steadily past them. Silas felt invisible beside the old man. Nobody seemed to notice them at all.

"People are in such a hurry nowadays," he remarked.

"They always have been," Job said. "You just don't notice how fast they move until you have nothing to do and nowhere to be."

Silas spotted a middle-aged woman in the crowd and smiled up at her hopefully. She shot him an icy look and hurried by. "It's not even that they don't see us," he observed. "It's that they don't want to see us."

"I don't mind it," Job said. "I force people to think about the things they'd otherwise rather forget. They can choose to ignore me, but that doesn't change the fact that they've seen me."

"The world is cold," Silas said.

"Damned cold," Job agreed. "But all I can do is sit here and watch it go by. Sitting, watching, and waiting—that's what my life has reduced itself to."

"What are you waiting for?"

"Death."

Silas was certain he had misheard. "Sorry?"

"I'm waiting to die," Job said. "Oh, don't look so surprised. What else can somebody like me wait for?"

"I don't know," Silas said. "Another day?"

"Another day of what—sitting, watching, and waiting?" The old man coughed into the folds of his blanket. "No, thank you."

Silas studied the blanket silently. There were more holes in it than he could count. "How long have you had that?" he asked.

"For as long as I've been homeless," Job said. "About three years."

"You've been homeless for three years?"

"That's right."

"I'm sorry," Silas said, and he meant it. For the past three years, the university atop the hill had been his home.

"That's life," Job said. "There's nothing to be sorry about."

Silas shook his head. He slipped off his rucksack and rummaged through it while Job watched him warily. At length, he pulled out two flannel shirts and a pair of woolen socks and laid them across his lap. He had packed them as extras for the weekend, but he realized now that he had brought along far more than he actually needed.

"Here," he said, folding them up together and presenting them to the old man. "I don't know if they'll fit you, but at least they'll keep you warm."

"I can't take those," Job said immediately.

"Why not?"

"Look at them! They're too nice. I'll just get them dirty."

"Then get them dirty," Silas said. "They're yours now."

"I'll ruin them," Job protested. "Go on—put them away."

"They don't belong to me anymore," Silas said. "They're yours now." He handed the clothes to Job, who accepted them hesitantly.

Job turned the bundle over in his hands. "Are you sure about this?"

"Absolutely," Silas said.

He watched as the old man unfurled the flannels, one after the other, and separated the socks with care. Deep within his tired eyes, a light flickered to life. He broke into a toothless grin and clasped Silas's hand. "Thank you," he whispered.

Silas patted his arm. "You're welcome," he said. "You stay warm, all right?"

"I'll try," Job said. "God knows I always try." He shivered beneath his blanket. "It's just so *damned* cold..."

"I know," Silas said, weary of the truth. "I know."

He rose to his feet, wished Job well, and returned his rucksack to his back. Once more, he set his gaze on the distant horizon, trying to ignore the fact that he was rejoining the frigid crowd.

IV

Before long, Silas reached the train station. He let the rushing river of eager travelers carry him down the slanted staircase, through the clacking turnstiles, and into the bustling depot. He found his way to the correct platform and checked his watch beneath a yawning brick archway. The train was five minutes away.

He leaned against the wall and crossed his arms, contemplating the barren tracks. As he waited, he observed a young couple standing a short distance away. The man was clad in a dirt-colored overcoat and a shabby pair of fingerless gloves. He had the alabaster features of a Renaissance statue, which complicated his rat-like demeanor. The girl was blonde-haired and blue-eyed, and was clutching a handkerchief embroidered with roses. Her shoulders were trembling, and Silas realized she was crying.

"But why?" she was saying to the rat-faced man. "Why won't you stay?"

"I already told you," he said stiffly. "I'm not going to change my mind."

"Please," she sniffed. "Don't do this. Don't go."

"I have to," the rat-faced man said. "It's not the same anymore, and you know it."

"Rich, darling!" The girl's sapphire eyes were shimmering with tears, but he refused to meet them. "Haven't I been good to you?"

"You've been fine," Rich mumbled. "But it's finished now. I've moved on."

"Well, I haven't!"

"I know. But I think it's time you do."

The girl dabbed her eyes with her rose-embroidered handkerchief. "You used to tell me you loved me," she said quietly. "Do you remember that?"

Rich took a step away from her and looked impatiently toward the tracks. Silas checked his watch. The train was only three minutes away. He could hear its whistle shrieking in the distance.

"You used to tell me lots of nice things," she continued. "What happened to us, darling?"

"Things changed," Rich said tersely.

"When? How?"

"It doesn't matter. It's over now."

"Rich—"

"No. It's finished."

"Rich, please—"

"It's finished, I said. I've moved on."

"But I—"

"Listen," Rich said sharply. "I'm done talking about it. It's finished. I don't know why you followed me here. You're making a damned fool of yourself."

The girl clutched her handkerchief and wept as though he had struck her. Rich looked toward the tracks once more and sighed with relief as the platform began to shudder. Silas could hear the train rattling toward them. Soon, the gleaming black engine pulled into the station.

"I'm leaving now," Rich said, and the girl cried louder. He turned his back on her and strode off without delay.

Silas made ready to cross the platform and board the train, but the girl's sobs had him frozen beneath the archway. He approached her slowly, unsure of exactly what to say. She was a rose without thorns, stripped of her petals and her dignity.

"Are you all right?" he asked, even though he already knew the answer.

The girl bowed her head. "How much did you hear?"

"I heard enough."

She swallowed with difficulty. "I was such a fool."

He said nothing, then opened his arms. The girl stepped into them and wept against his overcoat. He grimaced, rubbing her back in somber silence.

"I'll never let him go," she whispered. "I feel so cold..."

"I'm sorry," Silas said.

He held her for a moment longer before going off to board the train. The girl's tears lingered on the shoulder of his overcoat, but he let them stay. They turned to ice as he handed his rucksack to one of the porters and climbed onto the long, black car.

He squeezed his way down the cramped aisle, searching for an open seat. With a start, he noticed the rat-faced man sitting by himself and asked if anyone was sitting next to him. The rat-faced man shook his head.

Silas sat. "Damned cold out there, isn't it?"

The rat-faced man shrugged. "It's not that bad." He put out his hand, giving Silas a glimpse of the dirt beneath his fingernails. "Rich."

Silas shook the hand, surprised by how limp it was. "Silas."

The train lurched forward, and Rich settled back in his seat. He plucked a cigarette from the breast pocket of his overcoat and tapped the end of it on his knee. "I'd offer you one," he said, "but I'm running low as it is. I hope you don't mind."

"It's no trouble," Silas said. "I don't smoke, anyway."

"I don't blame you," Rich said, lighting the cigarette between his teeth. "It's a nasty habit, but I've given up trying to fight it. The temptation gets to me, every time." He blew a cloud of smoke at the window. "Ah, well. We all have our vices."

A sharply-dressed attendant arrived to check their tickets. "How far away is Freedman's Notch?" Silas asked him.

The attendant validated their tickets with his silver holepunch. "That's at the end of the line," he said. "Twelve stops away. We'll arrive there this evening."

Silas thanked him and he was gone.

Rich took a drag from his cigarette. "What are you doing in Freedman's Notch?"

"I'm spending the weekend in the mountains."

"Yeah? I'm sure it'll be damned cold."

"I'm sure. Where are you headed?"

Rich leered. "I'm seeing a girl in Colchester," he said. "I've been writing her for weeks now. She's real fine."

"That's nice," Silas said, thinking immediately of the girl with the rose-embroidered handkerchief.

Rich nodded. "What about you—talked to any girls lately?"

"I talked to one this morning, actually," Silas said. "I think you may have known her. She was crying, back at the platform."

Rich took another drag from his cigarette and massaged his temples. "Ugh," he said. "*That* one. What did she tell you?"

"Not much. She told me she'd never let you go."

"Of course, she did. What did you tell her?"

"I told her I was sorry." Silas sighed. "She's hurting, Rich. She's heartbroken."

Rich rolled his cigarette between his thumb and index finger. "She's been heartbroken since the beginning," he said. "That much has never changed."

"What do you mean?"

"When I met her," Rich said, "she had just been left by another man. A real sad sap, from what she told me. He never consummated anything." He blew a cloud of smoke and leered. "Ah, well. Made things easier for me."

Silas narrowed his eyes through the haze. "You went through with it?" he said. "Even though you knew she was broken?"

"Of course, I did," Rich said. "I couldn't have asked to meet her at a better time. I was nice to her and she fell for me overnight. Gave me everything I wanted. Everything and more." He sucked on his cigarette. "It's a damned shame I got bored."

"You got bored?"

"Yes, and I told her that."

"Don't you think that's a little harsh?"

"No. It was the truth. I don't know what else she would have wanted me to say."

The train came to a screeching stop and a wave of people got off. Rich finished his cigarette and dipped into his breast pocket for another. "I don't know," he said. "Things were fine for a few months, but then they got stale. She just didn't thrill me anymore."

"When did you start writing the girl from Colchester?" Silas asked.

"Which one?"

"What do you mean, 'which one?' The one you were just telling me about."

"Sorry." Rich lit a fresh cigarette as the train started moving again. "There have been a lot of girls from Colchester. It's a grand place. Ever been there?"

"No." Silas squinted through the smoke once more. "When did you start writing the latest girl?"

"About a month ago. But before her..." Rich whistled. "There have been a *lot*."

"All of this while you were with the girl at the platform?"

"All of this while I was with the girl at the platform," he affirmed. "Let me tell you—it wasn't easy. I've ridden this route by moonlight more times than I can count."

Silas grimaced, conscious of the tearstains on his overcoat. "You're not serious."

"You know I am."

"Did she ever find out?"

"No. Never." Rich smirked at the words, letting his cigarette hang from his mouth. "And to add to the fact, after I told her I was bored, she asked what she could do to get me to stay. She offered me every-thing—even offered to let me have other girls if it meant I wouldn't leave her."

"What did you tell her?"

"I told her I'd be bored, all the same. But I don't know, maybe I should've stayed. It was a pretty good arrangement—her by day and the others by night." He shrugged. "Ah, well. No sense in regretting it now."

Silas said nothing. Rich took a puff from his cigarette, then went on.

"No, I think I would've regretted it if I had stayed," he said. "It was such a chore to keep things going. You don't know how many times I had to say it before she finally gave me what I wanted."

"How many times you had to say what?"

"That I loved her."

"You told her you loved her?"

"I had to," he said. "She wouldn't agree to anything unless I did. You know how stubborn girls can be."

Silas swallowed, starting to feel nauseous. He figured it was the smoke. "Well, did you?"

"Did I what?"

"Did you love her?"

Rich leered through the haze. "No," he said. "Of course not. But I said what I had to say."

Silas shut his eyes and coughed in the direction of his shoulder. All he could think about were the girl's tears. "You really hurt her."

"Who? The girl at the platform?"

"Yes—the one you left crying."

"No, I didn't. I told you, she was broken when I met her."

"She may have been broken," Silas said, "but now she's shattered. You took what she had left and smashed it all to pieces. Now what does she have?"

Rich looked out the window, noiselessly nursing his cigarette. The train had begun to slow. They had arrived in Colchester.

"She has nothing," Silas answered for him. "She's cold and alone."

Rich exhaled a cloud of smoke. "Too bad."

"What?"

"Too bad." He extinguished what was left of his cigarette, flicking it into the ashtray by his armrest. "I got what I wanted, and now I'm moving on."

Silas stared. "You're a bastard."

"No, I take what I want. You have to nowadays."

"No, you don't."

"Yes, you do. Everybody does."

"I don't," Silas said. "I'm glad I don't. You're a goddamned bastard."

The train came to a complete stop. Rich stood and weaseled his way out into the aisle, flashing his rat-like leer.

"Ah, well," he said. "At least I'm happy."

"It's a damned shame you are."

He shrugged, then turned away. Silas watched him go without a word.

V

He spent the rest of the trip alone, staring out the window in jaded silence. The majority of the other passengers got off right after Rich, headed in for their shifts at the mills and factories. The rest got off in St. Albans, or just beyond in Swanton Junction. Not long afterward, the train crossed the lake on a narrow granite causeway. The trees thickened considerably on the other side, enclosing the tracks within a deep and snowy wilderness. It was almost twilight when the train finally emerged from the forest and came to a long-awaited halt in Freedman's Notch.

There was hardly anybody at the lonely station, and all of the accompanying offices were dark. Silas accepted his rucksack from the porter and took in the view from the platform. The u-shaped valley lay beyond, a bone-white gash in the rambling horizon.

"Is there an inn nearby?" he asked him. He had planned on posing the question to the station's concierge, but there didn't appear to be one.

The porter frowned, then pointed vaguely toward the darkening valley. "I think so," he said. "If there is, it shouldn't be far from here—not more than a mile into the Notch."

"Thanks," Silas said, and handed him a tip. He seemed eager to get out of the cold.

As the train shrieked and rattled away, Silas freed his snowshoes from his rucksack and secured them to his feet. He pulled the straps tight and straightened up, taking a grateful breath of mountain air. It was cold like the air in the city, but it smelled far cleaner and felt much less confined. He waited awhile before pulling on his hat and mittens, letting the wind wash over his city-spawned woes. They had accumulated steadily since the crash—chilling his blood, numbing his mind, and leaving his conscience encased in ice.

He wondered if the scowling man was still scowling and if he ever smiled. He wondered if the waiter ever grew tired of waiting, and if the café had ever considered starting a breadline. He prayed for the end of the breadlines, ever-aware of the cold world they represented, and hoped that the unemployed would soon find an escape from their shame. He thought of the people who had lost everything while he had lost nothing—people like Job, who sat huddled alone on a street corner while the frigid crowds shuffled past. He wondered if Job had gotten rid of that horrible threadbare blanket, if he had perhaps fashioned a new one out of the two flannel shirts that he could now call his own. He wondered if his new pair of woolen socks was pulled over his frostbitten hands or hugging his weary feet. Regardless of the purpose they currently served, he was happy to have provided them.

He wondered if tears still streaked the face of the girl at the platform and regretted the fact that he had not been able to comfort her for very long. He knew that the cold had already taken its toll on her, that there wasn't much else he could have said or done, but her sorrow weighed on him nonetheless. He fumed at the memory of Rich's rat-like leer, cringing at the lingering odor of cigarette smoke that clung to his overcoat in the wind.

I'll never let him go, the girl had said, but Silas sincerely hoped that she would. It would take time for her to move on, but her winter would persist for as long as she refused to let him go. Even after she did that, there was no guarantee that the ice in her heart would ever truly thaw. Roses were hardy, but even they could be smothered by the snow.

Silas shook his head ruefully and took a deep breath. The world was cold, and the cold was cruel—but he'd be damned if things on this side of the lake weren't at least a little bit warmer. He had been yearning for this escape since the crash, and now that he had it, he was determined to enjoy it. He stepped off the platform and onto the unplowed road, trekking off in the direction of the mountains.

The sky was indigo by the time he reached Freedman's Notch, and the snow was sparkling in the starlight. The valley's sloping headwalls rushed to meet each other in the dark, joining together in sweeping parabolic unity. Dense rows of stately evergreens loomed around the road, sagging beneath the white weight of their bristling boughs. The air had grown colder, but there was warmth in the woodsmoke drifting above the trees. Silas located the source of the smoke at a bend in the road: a modest log cabin with candles flickering in its windows. He trudged up to the door and knocked on its weathered surface. The floor creaked from within, and the door swung open.

A young woman smiled at him from the threshold. She wore a simple black dress and faded leather boots. Her hair was long and brown and tangled, like a wild horse's mane. She brushed it out of her bright blue eyes and ushered him inside.

Silas closed the door behind him and shivered. "Cold out there tonight," he remarked, shaking the snow from his overcoat.

The young woman laughed. "Welcome to Freedman's Notch," she said. "This is about as cold as it gets."

Silas checked his watch and hesitated. "I know it's late," he said, "but I'm hoping there's still vacancy..."

"There's plenty," the young woman assured him. "How long are you planning on staying?"

"Just for the weekend," Silas said. He unlaced his boots, which were still secured to his snowshoes, and left them on the doormat. "My train leaves at noon on Sunday."

"That's fine," the young woman said. "We can arrange a work-for-stay agreement, or you can pay up-front. I know times are hard."

"It's no trouble at all," Silas said, feeling somewhat guilty. He withdrew the money from the inner pocket of his overcoat. The wad of dollars was still just as thick.

She tucked the money away without counting it. "Go ahead and get settled in," she said, directing him up the stairs. "Any room you'd like."

"Thanks very much," Silas said. He made his way up the uneven staircase, which was scantily lit by the sconces on the wall. He chose a room with an owl carved into the door and laid his rucksack at the foot of the bed. It was a quaint space with a view that looked out over the snowy evergreens. The nightstand was home to a gas lantern and a dusty stack of books. Silas glanced at a few of the titles and saw that a few of them were by Thoreau. *Very fitting*, he thought.

He hung his overcoat on one of the bedposts and went back downstairs to find the young woman waiting for him. "I'm Vera," she said.

Silas shook her hand. Her grasp was warmer and much less delicate than he had expected. "Silas," he said.

"Come in," Vera said, beckoning for him to follow. She showed him into the inn's main room, which was divided down the middle by a long table. One half of the room was occupied by a modest kitchen; the other by a sizeable sitting area. A fire was blazing in the hearth.

"Warm yourself up," she said. "Are you hungry? I'm just about to serve dinner."

At the mention of food, Silas's stomach gave a low growl. "Dinner sounds terrific," he said.

Vera lifted a steaming pot from the stove and carried it to a corner of the table. "Bowls and spoons are in the cupboard," she said, nodding back toward the kitchen.

Silas went to fetch them and paused at the counter. "How many?"

"Just two," she said. "It's only you and me tonight."

He returned to the table. "I'm the only guest?"

Vera nodded. "I thought I'd be eating alone until you came knocking on my door." She ladled stew into his bowl and handed it back to him. It smelled strongly of rosemary and thyme.

"Is it usually this slow?" Silas said.

"Not usually," Vera said. "Well, it's always slow in the winter. The cold drives people away. But this..." She trailed off, ladling stew into her bowl. "This is definitely different. You're the first guest we've had in weeks."

"Really?" Silas said. "It's been that bad?"

"It's been difficult," she admitted. "Even in the warmer months, the crowds are thinning. People just don't have the money to spend anymore. Times are hard."

"The world is cold," Silas said with a sigh. He looked around the room and offered her half a smile. "But it feels much warmer in here."

Vera smiled back. "I hope so. I try my best to keep it warm."

Silas gestured to the wall above the mantle, where a painting of an owl was watching them eat. "Who's this little fellow?" he asked. "I thought you said I was the only guest."

Vera laughed. "Don't worry," she said. "You are. He's more of a permanent resident. My handsome little sentinel..."

"He's magnificent," Silas said, remembering the carving of the owl on the door upstairs. "You really like owls, don't you?"

"I love them," she said. "They're so wise. They know the world, and they know themselves." She beamed up at the painting. "I hope you get to see him while you're here. He's shy, you know. He doesn't always come around."

"You've seen him?" Silas said.

"Of course, I have. I couldn't have painted something that well from memory."

Silas gaped at the painting, then back at her. "*You* painted that?"

"That's right," Vera said. "He made a lousy model, though—always flying away when the light was right."

"He's marvelous," Silas said, immediately becoming aware of the other paintings on the walls. There were dozens of them—breathtaking renditions of flora and fauna, meticulously immortalized on canvas. "Did you do all of these?"

"Each and every one," Vera said. "I had to find something to do, with the inn being so slow. Painting keeps me smiling. It brings me peace."

"You do excellent work," Silas said, swallowing a mouthful of stew. He tapped his spoon on the edge of his bowl. "This is excellent, too."

"Thanks," Vera said, growing pink from the praise. "They're very simple things, really."

"Simplicity is undervalued," Silas said. "Have you tried selling these? I know people would buy them."

"I have," Vera admitted. "But the last time I tried, none of them sold."

"I don't believe it," Silas said.

Vera shrugged. "I'm telling the truth. But then again, that was probably my fault. I shouldn't have sold them alongside a dozen horses. People use horses. They don't use paintings."

"Horses? What were you selling horses for?"

"It was a slow summer," Vera said, "so we auctioned them off in the fall. With the way things are, we couldn't afford to keep them."

"I'm sorry to hear that," Silas said.

"It's all right," Vera said. "The inn needed money. Before times got hard, we'd take guests up into the mountains on horseback. They were grand horses. I wish we didn't have to sell them. They were such a joy to have around."

"You sold them all?"

"We had to." She sighed. "But as for the paintings, I don't care if they sell or not. They make me happy, either way."

Silas's spoon scraped the bottom of his empty bowl. "Good," he said. "That's what's important."

Vera cleared his bowl away and moved the pot of stew back to the stove. She returned with a tarnished kettle and a pair of metal mugs. "Tea?"

"Please," Silas said, and she poured him a mug. He raised it to his lips and took a sip. It tasted pleasantly of peppermint.

"So, tell me," Vera said, lowering herself into the seat across from him. "Is this your first time in the mountains?"

Silas nodded. "For years, I've looked at them from across the lake, but they're even more beautiful up close." He took another sip of tea and smiled. "I've needed some time away from the state of things. It's really nice to be here."

"How is it across the lake?" she asked. "I can't say I've ever been."

Silas thought of the city—of the scowling and shamefaced men, frigid crowds, and rat-faced drifters. "It's cold," he said. "Damned cold. Colder than it is here."

Vera raised an eyebrow. "Colder than it is here? I doubt that."

"It's a different kind of cold," he said. "It's harsh and constricting, and after a while, it really starts to weigh on you." He set his half-empty mug on the table and sighed.

Vera studied his face with kind eyes, then filled his mug to the brim. "I'm sure it's nice to get away," she said gently.

"It is," Silas said. "The mountains are a nice distraction from it all."

"They're more than a distraction," Vera said. "Trust me. They do wonders for the mind. They heal the heart and soothe the soul."

"I hope you're right," Silas said. His gaze wandered back to the painting of the owl above the mantle. "It's a wonder how owls stay warm in the cold. Well, maybe not—I'm sure their wings have something to do with it."

"I don't think it's their wings at all," Vera said thoughtfully.

"No?" Silas said. "What do you think it is?"

"I think it's their eyes."

"Their eyes?"

"Yes, their eyes."

"I think you're crazy," Silas said.

Vera shrugged. "Owls have such wise eyes. They see more of the world than we give them credit for."

Silas frowned. "What does that have to do with them being able to withstand the cold?"

Vera paused. A light was gleaming in her bright blue eyes. "Everything," she said at last.

"What?" Silas said.

Vera shrugged again, raising her mug of tea. "Welcome to Freedman's Notch," she said, with mystifying simplicity. "This is about as cold as it gets."

Silas laughed and touched his mug against hers. He supposed it didn't matter, anyway. He was happy and he was warm—here, in the mountains at last.

VI

Silas spent the night beneath a heavy patchwork quilt and awoke the next morning with the sunlight on his face. He dressed, shouldered his rucksack, and wandered downstairs. He found Vera near the hearth, standing behind an old easel. She held a paintbrush in one hand and a palette of paints in the other. A mason jar of cloudy water sat on the table nearby.

"Good morning," she said, looking up from the canvas. "Breakfast is on the table, if you're hungry."

Silas reached for a biscuit from the cloth-lined basket near the mason jar. It was still warm. "Thanks," he said, peering curiously at the easel. "What are you painting?"

"Come see," Vera said, stepping back from her work. "It's not finished yet though, so be kind."

Silas smiled at the landscape before him. He recognized the view immediately—the sweeping, sunlit slopes of the mountains that formed Freedman's Notch. "It's beautiful as it is," he said. "What else is there to add?"

"It needs depth," she said. "It needs shadows. You can't have light without shadows." She prodded her chin with the end of her brush. "I'd set up my easel outside the Notch if it was warmer. I could really use the perspective. I've painted everything from memory so far, so I know I'm missing something."

Silas slathered his biscuit with jam and took a bite. "It's pretty impressive, what you have already."

"It's decent right now," Vera said. "But I'm not satisfied with it yet. I've stared at this view for almost twenty years, but still—I know there's something I'm forgetting."

"You've lived here for twenty years?"

"Eighteen," she said. "I grew up here."

"That's grand," Silas said. "Alone?"

"Not always," Vera said, "but most of the time, yes. My parents were never around, so my grandfather raised me." She sighed. "I don't see much of him nowadays, either."

Silas nodded sorrowfully. "My condolences."

"Oh, he's not dead," Vera said. "He just loves his freedom. I think it makes him feel young again."

"What do you mean?"

"He's a backpacker," she explained. "A rambler. A regular old man of the mountains. No matter the month, no matter the season—he's out there, trekking down every trail."

Silas took a bite of his biscuit and chewed, wide-eyed. "You mean he's out there right now, in the dead of winter?"

Vera nodded. "The cold never really seemed to bother him. I've always admired that."

"Hiking every day, from sunrise to sunset," Silas mused. "It sounds terrific—well, with the exception of the cold."

"It's wonderful," Vera said softly. "We'd go backpacking all the time when I was younger. Nothing ever felt so free. He and I would hike up to a snowy ridge, camp below the summit, and watch the auroras dance across the sky."

Silas marveled at her word-woven image. "Do the two of you still hike together?" he asked.

"Not really," Vera said. "I stay behind and run the inn so that he can ramble and roam."

"All year?"

"Only during the winter," she said. "He comes back to run the inn during the summer. That's when I get my fill of the mountains."

Silas recalled the summertime view from the lake. "They've always looked stunning from across the water," he said. "Where do you usually hike?"

"Everywhere," Vera said simply. "All of the trails connect, in one way or another. Some of the mountains don't have trails, so I make my own. I carry my life around in a rucksack and hike where my heart takes me. It's an absolute dream, living that way. You feel free—like you've finally gotten away from it all."

"That sounds fantastic," Silas said. "Heading off into the mountains and leaving everything behind..." He contemplated her painting of the Notch. "I wish I could do that now. I could use an escape from the cold."

"I don't know if you can escape from the cold," Vera said.

"What?" Silas said. "Why not?"

"I don't know," she said. "It sounds nice, but I don't think it's as simple as leaving everything behind. I think the cold follows you wherever you go."

"Maybe you're right," Silas said. "But I'll be damned if I don't try to escape it by taking to the trail anyway."

Vera raised an eyebrow. "By yourself?"

"I don't see why not," he said.

"No," she said. "You'd be a fool to face the mountains alone."

"Then I won't go alone," he said. "I'll go with you. We can escape together. You know the mountains better than anybody."

Vera laughed. "I wouldn't say *that*," she said.

"Oh, don't be modest," Silas said. "You wouldn't have gotten anywhere with this painting if you didn't know them so well."

"Well," Vera said, "I suppose I do know them somewhat well. Walking among them is like visiting with old friends."

"Then it's settled," Silas said. "We'll hike off into the mountains and make our escape—and the cold will be none the wiser."

Vera laughed again, then sighed and shook her head. "You're joking," she said. "I know you're joking. But I really wish it was that simple."

Silas took the final bite of his biscuit, realizing numbly that it had lost its taste. "So do I."

Vera stared hard at her painting, as though trying to convince herself of its bright and sunny reality. She pursed her lips, then rested the end of her brush against her chin.

"What is it?" Silas asked.

"I'm wondering if you'd like to take a walk with me..."

"Certainly," he said. "Where?"

"Beyond the Notch," Vera said. "Through the forest, and up a mountain." She nodded at his rucksack, then pointed in the direction of the snowshoes he had left by the door. "You have everything you need, but let me be your guide. I'll show you the way."

Silas grinned and tightened the straps of his rucksack. "Let's make our escape."

"Follow me," Vera said, her blue eyes glimmering. "The mountains are waiting."

VII

They laced up their boots, secured snowshoes to their soles, and stepped out into the winter sunlight. The air was crisp, the sky was clear, and the snow on the twisting road crunched beneath their feet. The wind steered them into the Notch, threading its icy fingers through their hair. Silas gazed up at the snow-sculpted headwalls, awed by their untamed grandeur. Vera patted his arm fondly.

"What?" he said.

"You," she said, smiling. "Sometimes I forget you're experiencing all of this for the first time."

"It's lovely," he said. "Just like your painting..."

"It's far lovelier than my painting," Vera said. "The mountains are Mother Nature's masterpiece. She's the best artist I know."

Silas gawked at them, suspended in a silent stupor. Vera nudged him playfully. "Come on," she said. "There's so much more to see."

She led him off the road and into the trees, where the snow was softer and deeper. They plodded alongside the ice-encased banks of a gurgling stream. Its coursing water was ghostly and green, like the liquified essence of a shimmering aurora. Silas was mesmerized.

"Deidre Brook," Vera said. "Eighteen winters in this Notch, and I've never seen it freeze."

"Not even once?"

She shook her head. "Not even once. If I didn't know any better, I'd say it was made of the cold."

They hiked on. Deidre Brook meandered beside them. Silas listened to the rushing water. It was babbling aloud in a language he didn't understand, but it seemed to have something to say.

"Silas," Vera said suddenly. "Would you like to hear a story?"

"All right," he said.

"I'll warn you now: it's rather cold."

"The world is cold," he said, undeterred. "Let's hear it."

With a deep breath, Vera began. "Once, many years ago," she said, "a hunter was wandering through a wild mountain valley. He was a proud man, too proud to admit that he had lost his way, and he carried a gun to show the world that he was unafraid. He stumbled across a cabin in the woods and made arrangements with the owner to stay for the night."

"A wild mountain valley," Silas repeated slowly. "By that, do you mean Freedman's Notch?"

She appeared not to have heard him. "The owner of the cabin had a daughter," she continued. "She was a blossoming flower, a rose with primped petals and filed-down thorns. The hunter was brusque and bitter to her, but she fell in love with him nonetheless. She felt comforted by his gun and gave him everything he ever wanted. Ultimately, his one-night stay turned into a yearlong sojourn, and he asked the owner of the cabin for his daughter's hand in marriage."

"Bold move," Silas said with a chuckle. "What did the cabin owner think of that?"

"He was reluctant at first," Vera said. "He had his doubts about the hunter's intentions, having seen over the years what men with guns could do. But he cared very deeply about his daughter's happiness and let the wedding proceed. The rose was pleased, but..." She trailed off, slowing her pace.

"But what?"

She drew to a halt. "But the hunter's satisfaction was waning."

Silas stopped beside her. "Waning?"

"He began to feel trapped by his rose's affection," Vera said. "He longed once more for the open woods and regretted coming to the valley in the first place. At length, he decided to leave. On a cold winter's night, he packed up his gun and left the cabin behind."

Silas was immediately reminded of the rat-faced man from the train. He scowled, remembering his icy leer. "That bastard," he spat.

Vera lowered her gaze to the brook, which was flowing with furious urgency. "The hunter's rose was shattered," she said. "She set out after him, in spite of her father's advice, and tried to trace his trail. It was snowing in the valley that night. The cold had covered his tracks. She searched everywhere for her lost love, but it was no use. He had gone, and she was alone."

Silas grimaced, touching the shoulder of his overcoat. There were still tearstains there—the anguished, unfading legacy of the girl at the platform. "That bastard," he said again. "That selfish, heartless bastard..."

Vera was quiet for a moment. "The rose," she said. "Her name was Deidre. Her father found her the next day, frozen to death by this brook."

Silas stared down at the murmuring water. "That's the coldest story I've ever heard," he said.

Vera reached for his hand and squeezed it gently. Her grasp was kind and warm. "This way," she said, pulling him away from the brook's edge. "There's something else I want you to see."

She showed him into an evergreen glade, where the snow was sprinkled with faded green needles. In the middle of the clearing, at the base of a towering cedar, lay a single weathered headstone. Much of its surface was obscured by the snow, but Silas could still make out the name.

"*Deidre Nancy Barton*," he read, then cleared some of the snow away. "*Died February 15, 1915...*"

"Seventeen years ago, this month," Vera said. "Here, at the foot of this tree."

"That's her, then? The hunter's rose?"

"That's her," Vera whispered. "A fallen flower, laid to rest beneath the snow. Cold and dormant, but lovely as ever."

Silas bowed his head. "May she rest in peace."

They departed from the clearing and headed north, tramping through knee-deep banks of sugary snow. Before long, the trees thickened and the trail led uphill. After a steep stretch of climbing, they crested the ridge and wandered out onto a granite ledge. A vast evergreen expanse was spread out beneath them.

Again, Vera squeezed his hand. "What do you think?"

Silas beamed at the endless panorama, shading his eyes from the sun. "Unbelievable," he said. He noticed the lake, glinting like an enormous frozen mirror, on the distant horizon. "I feel free."

"I know the feeling," she said. "Wonderful, isn't it?"

Silas sighed, squinting at the lake. He couldn't see the sprawling city on its opposite shore, but he knew it was there, bitterly awaiting his return. "Do you mind if I stay up here awhile?" he asked.

"Not at all," she said. "Is everything all right?"

"Yes, of course. Everything's fine."

"No, really—I can tell it's not. What's wrong?"

"It's nothing."

Vera bit her lip. "Was it the story?"

He shook his head.

"I'm sorry," she said. "I told you it was cold..."

"It's not that," Silas said.

"Then what is it?"

He gestured to the view before them, his eyes fixed on the lake.

"It's just so beautiful up here," he said. "I finally feel like I'm away from it all. I guess I'm trying to make the most of my escape."

She followed his gaze. "From the cold?"

He nodded and the lake winked at him. "I don't really want to go back."

They braced themselves against a frigid gust of wind. When it subsided, Vera rubbed his arm.

"Silas?"

"Yes, Vera?"

"How do owls stay warm in the cold?"

"With their wings?"

"No," she said. "With their eyes."

He managed a laugh. "I still think you're crazy."

She shrugged, then rubbed his arm again. "Take all the time you need up here. When you're ready, follow my tracks back to the inn. I'll have tea waiting for you."

"Thanks," he said. "Thanks a lot."

She left him with the warmth of her gaze, then turned and disappeared below the frosted timberline.

VIII

Silas stood on the ledge for some time, quietly contemplating the view. The pale blue sky was free of clouds and the sun bathed the sweeping snowscape in golden light. The surrounding ridge was jagged with icy crags that peered down into the Notch below. It thrilled him to think that these were the same peaks he had once gazed at from across the lake. Finally, he was among them—far away from Burlington's scowling, shivering crowds. He savored the silence of the mountaintop, grateful for the breadth of its peaceful panorama.

There was a sudden scuffling from behind him, and he turned to see an old backpacker with grizzled hair regaining his footing on the bedrock. "Damned ice," he puffed, clacking forward in a well-worn pair of snowshoes. Silas moved over to share the ledge with him.

"Nice day, isn't it?" the old backpacker said.

"Beautiful day," Silas said. "Cold, but beautiful."

The old backpacker shrugged. "I don't mind the cold," he said. "Not when I have views like this to keep me warm."

"This is unbelievable," Silas agreed.

"If you think this is nice," the old backpacker said, "then you should see some of the views from across the Notch."

Silas surveyed the mountains in the distance. "What are they like?"

The old backpacker whistled through his teeth. "Gorgeous," he said. "Stark, snowy, and dead quiet. I love them that way."

"They must be cold, too."

"Extremely cold," the old backpacker said. "Cold enough to turn your blood to ice. But like I said, I don't mind it. I've spent so many winters in this Notch that it hardly bothers me anymore."

Silas considered him for a moment. "You're Vera's grandfather, aren't you?"

The old backpacker smiled. "I am," he said, extending a mittened hand. "Call me Ernest."

"Pleasure," Silas said. The handshake was firm and warm. "I'm Silas."

"You must be staying at the inn," Ernest said. "What's it like these days? I haven't been there since the fall."

"It's fantastic," Silas said. "Really fantastic. Vera's been a fine host. She's a talented painter and an even better friend."

"It warms me to hear that, son. How long are you staying?"

"Not for long, unfortunately. My train leaves tomorrow at noon." Silas glanced at the lake on the horizon. "But I'm glad I came out here. I've been needing some time away from home."

"Where's home?"

Silas pointed at the lake. "There's a city on the opposite shore," he said. "Burlington. I study at the university there."

"How do you like it?"

"The university's nice," Silas said. "But the city's very cold."

"I never cared much for the city," Ernest said. "Neither did my father. That's why we moved here. The inn you're staying at was my childhood home."

"It's a grand place."

"Thanks, son. It was built by my father."

"Was it?"

"Yes, sir. He was a great man—a trail-seasoned veteran of the Civil War. He came to the mountains searching for peace."

"Did he find it?"

"He did. And he found something else, too."

"What's that?"

"The truth," Ernest said. "He learned that the mountains were just as cold as the city, and just as cold as the frosted fields of Gettysburg. The chill followed him wherever he went."

"The world is cold," Silas concluded with a sigh.

"Hm," Ernest said, pondering the view. "How did you find your way up here? There's scarcely a trail. I bushwhacked up from the east."

Silas furrowed his brow, trying to remember. "Vera brought me up from the south, I think."

"Ah, yes—from the Notch road. You must have followed the brook."

"We did," he recalled. "Then we passed through a clearing and started to climb. We climbed, and climbed—"

"And climbed some more." Ernest chuckled. "That's a steep route. Densely wooded, too."

"Yes, but Vera had no trouble finding her way. She's an excellent guide."

"She's a damned good guide," Ernest said proudly. "I taught her everything she knows."

"Well then, you taught her well," Silas said. "The mountains are her closest friends."

Ernest grinned. "What else would you expect? She's a Barton. The mountains are in her blood."

Silas blinked. In a flash of memory, he saw the surname etched into the headstone by the brook. "She's a Barton?" he said.

"She sure is," Ernest said. "We both are."

"You don't say. Did you ever know Deidre?"

In an instant, Ernest's smile faded away. "How do you know that name?"

"Vera told me the story," Silas explained. "It's terrible—one of the coldest I've ever heard."

Ernest looked down at his snowshoes. His eyes mirrored the frozen surface of the lake on the horizon.

"Did you ever know her?" Silas asked again.

Slowly, Ernest nodded. "Deidre was my daughter," he said quietly.

Silas froze. "What?"

"She was my daughter," he repeated. "My rose. I buried her by the brook that now bears her name."

Silas stared. His eyes began to water in the cold, and he willed himself to blink. "I'm sorry," he said. It was the only thing he could think to say.

Ernest lifted his gaze to the view beyond. There were many tired lines in his weathered face. "It's all right," he said. "It's seventeen winters in the past. Doesn't always feel that way, but it's what I have to tell myself."

Silas's mind was numb. Immediately, he thought of Vera and rubbed his eyes. "Wait," he said. "If you're Vera's grandfather, and Deidre was your daughter, then wouldn't that mean that—"

"Deidre was Vera's mother," Ernest finished. "Yes, it would."

"Which means that the hunter from the story—"

"That rotten *bastard* of a hunter was Vera's father. Yes, you're right about that, too."

"I wish I wasn't," Silas said. "I wish he'd been a better man."

"To hell with him," Ernest snarled. "He abandoned the family that he never should have had and ran off to a town on the other side of the Notch. They found him dead in the street, murdered by sorrow and whisky. That rotten, rat-faced *bastard*..."

Silas scowled. "Good riddance."

"Good riddance," Ernest said. He took a deep breath, massaging his forehead. "I won't lie—I'm a little surprised that Vera told you all of that. That story carries a lot of pain for her. She hasn't told many people."

"Then why did she tell me?"

"I don't know. Maybe she thought you needed to hear it."

Silas paused, recalling Vera's kind eyes and radiant persona. "I don't understand it," he said, shaking his head. "I just don't understand it."

"You don't understand what?"

"Vera," he said. "I don't understand her. I really don't."

"What about her?"

"How is she so warm when her story is so cold?"

"She's a Barton," Ernest said. "She's resilient, like the rest of her family. Like I am. Like her mother was."

"Isn't there more to it than that?"

"She's strong, Silas. She's brave. Deidre was, too, but..." He trailed off. His gaze was fixed on the frozen lake.

Silas sighed. "But sometimes the world is just too cold."

"Yes," Ernest said. "Sometimes it is." He squinted up at the sun. "But sometimes it isn't."

"What do you mean?"

"Look around," he said. "The world is cold—but even in winter, the sun still shines. The birds still sing. The brooks still flow. The mountains still stand—and so do you and I." He tapped the summit with his snowshoe. "Look at us. We're here because of our own grit and spirit. There's something to be said about that. Don't you think?"

Silas was quiet for a moment. "I suppose you're right," he said.

Ernest nodded. "But you have more to say."

"I do—I'm just not sure if I want to say it."

"You might as well," Ernest encouraged. "Go on. You might as well."

"I don't know," Silas said. "I'm beginning to think I can't escape the cold. I've tried everything, but I don't think I can."

"You're right," Ernest said, after a pause. "You can't. What made you think you could?"

"I don't know," Silas said again. "I just really thought I could. Something inside me was convinced that I could run away to the mountains for a weekend and finally be rid of it. I thought I'd left it in Burlington, but it followed me across the lake."

"It'll follow you everywhere," Ernest said. "Especially to the mountains. Winter in the Notch is harsh and bitter. This is as cold as it gets."

"I've heard that before," Silas said. "Vera told me that last night, but I didn't really believe her." He shivered, recalling Deidre's headstone with frigid clarity. "I do now—I just wish it wasn't that way."

"Me, too," Ernest admitted.

"So, that's it, then?" Silas said. "You really can't escape the cold?"

Ernest shook his head. "That's it. You really can't."

"Not at all?"

"Not at all."

Silas felt his hopes turn to ice. "Have you ever tried?"

"Son, I've been trying for the last seventeen years," Ernest said. "And if there's one thing I've learned through all that time, it's that the cold will always be here."

Silas sighed, setting his eyes in the direction of the city. "Then I'm at a loss," he said. "I don't know what to do anymore."

"Stop trying to escape it," Ernest said.

"But how?" Silas said. "That's all I've ever done."

Ernest gestured down at their feet. "Lace up your hiking boots," he said. "Learn to live with it, like me."

"How do I do that?"

"Take a deep breath and turn away. Don't pay it any mind. The cold tends not to bother you if you pretend it isn't there."

Silas hesitated. The lake was looking him in the face. "I've never been good at ignoring things," he said.

"Well," Ernest said, "it's not too late to try. You may have blazed one trail for yourself, but you can always start hiking in another direction."

"It's difficult to change directions," Silas pointed out. "Especially when you've committed yourself to hiking one way all along."

Ernest patted Silas on the shoulder. His eyes were warm and wise. "Hike on, son. The mountains are only as cold as we make them out to be."

IX

Silas thanked Ernest and wished him well, taking one last look at the view from the ledge. He floundered down the snowy mountainside and through the dense forest, stopping momentarily in the midst of the evergreen glade. He rested a somber hand atop Deidre's headstone and shivered, cursing the cold under his breath.

Ernest had told him not to pay it any mind, but the chill was near-impossible to ignore. There was a part of him that believed he could ignore it, but the rest of him was reluctant to try. It felt colder to spurn it than it did to acknowledge it, and there was no warmth in his resulting discontent. He puzzled over Ernest's ability to withstand the cold, then patted Deidre's headstone and muttered a prayer. Upon leaving the clearing, he trudged alongside her babbling brook, listening intently to its ceaseless storytelling.

The water was coursing with grief, and Silas sensed its weight on his conscience. Winter's toll was never-ending. The world was full of loss, and he had seen so much of it. He had seen people without food, without jobs, without homes, and without dignity. He had seen them disrespected, disadvantaged, and disregarded by uncaring crowds. He had seen them used, shunned, and shattered by rat-faced men and their false promises of love.

He hung his head. The world was cold, and he had watched so

many people freeze. The truth was inescapable, and there was nothing he could do to change it.

As he located the unplowed road through the trees, he got to thinking about Vera. The first eighteen years of her life had been unforgivingly frigid, and yet during his visit, he had seldom seen her scowl. This perplexed him. If anyone could afford to scowl at the cruelty of the cold, it was her. Her past was bleak, but her eyes were benevolent and bright. Even after Ernest's explanation, he scarcely understood how.

At length, the road rounded a bend and the inn came into view. Silas let himself inside and left his snowshoes by the door. Deidre's daughter was standing behind her easel, paintbrush in hand. She beamed when he came in and crossed the room to give him a hug. Silas held her tight, surprised by how warm she was.

"You're cold," she remarked.

"You're not," he said.

They drew apart. Vera gestured to the sitting area in front of the hearth. "Go get warm by the fire," she said. "I'll pour you some tea."

He sank into an armchair and studied the familiar canvas on the easel. The sun within the painting was still shining, but the snowy slopes of the Notch were now austere with shadows.

She sat beside him, handing him a mug of steaming tea. "I think our little excursion did me good," she said, smiling proudly at her work. "I finally have some fresh memories to refer to."

"I can tell," Silas said. "You added shadows."

"You sound disappointed," Vera said. "What's wrong with them? Aren't they realistic?"

"There's nothing wrong with them," he said. "They're very realistic. They give you a much clearer sense of the cold."

She was watching him closely. "You're not warming up. Do I need to add another log to the fire?"

Silas shook his head. "The fire's fine."

"Then what is it?"

"Nothing," he said, looking down at his tea.

"All right. How was the mountaintop?"

"It was grand," Silas said. "Another hiker came along after you left—a regular old man of the mountains."

Slowly, Vera broke into a grin. "You don't mean—"

"It was him," Silas said. "I couldn't believe it myself."

"How was he?" she asked. "I haven't seen him since the fall."

"He was...thoughtful. We both were."

Vera pursed her lips. "What did you talk about?"

"All sorts of things."

"Like what?"

"The view. The cold. Where we've lived."

"Anything else?"

He swallowed. "We talked about Deidre."

"Oh." Vera's shoulders drooped. "And I'm guessing he told you a little bit more of her story than I did, didn't he?"

Silas met her gaze. "Why didn't you tell me?"

"I didn't want you to feel bad about it," she said. "I didn't want to add weight to the belief that you already hold."

"That the world is cold?"

"Yes."

"Why?"

She looked away. "Because it is," she said. "Sometimes it really is. The world can be cold and dark and sad."

Silas sighed. "I know."

"But," Vera said. "Sometimes it's not. Sometimes the world is warm and bright and happy. Far too often, people forget that." She paused. "You, especially."

"It can be an easy thing to forget in the dead of winter," Silas mumbled. "When the sky is gray and the wind is strong and the clouds block out the sun."

Vera contemplated the sunlight in her painting. "It isn't always that bleak."

"Maybe not here—but it is in the city."

"All the time?"

"Most of the time."

She nudged his leg with her foot. "Tell me more about that."

"About what?"

"The city. I want to know what it's like."

"It's full of unpleasant people," he said. "Angry, selfish, frigid people—but they're not the ones who suffer." He thought of the weary waiter, of the shamefaced and homeless men, and of the sobbing girl at the platform. "Good people get caught in the cold, Vera, and I can't do a thing to stop it. All I can do is watch them freeze."

Her gaze was sincere. "Go on."

"People are hurting," Silas said. "The economy is bad and the consequences are cruel. Times are harsh, but I'm hardly affected by them. I can afford not to be, and that really weighs on me."

"What do you mean by that?"

"I'm a university man. I come from money, and money is cold. I have more than enough of it, and I'm really sorry about that. But people don't want me to be sorry. They don't want me to feel bad for them, even though I still do. It's a damned terrible thing, watching them freeze and not being able to help them."

"Have you tried to help them?"

"Somewhat. I've offered them money, but they don't seem to want that sort of sympathy. The only thing they're apt to accept is a conversation—that's it."

"And what's wrong with that?"

"Well, it's just a conversation. It's not much of anything."

"But it's something."

"It's something—but it doesn't help much."

"I don't know," Vera said. "I think it does. I think a conversation is the kindest thing you can give someone. I think there's value in listening—in acknowledging that you understand."

"It still doesn't feel like enough," Silas said.

"What would feel like enough?"

He thought for a moment. "An end to the cold. I wish I could make it easier for people. I wish I could make it so they wouldn't freeze."

"It's not such a bad thing, to freeze," Vera said. "The forest freezes every winter, and it's reborn again every spring. The cold builds resilience. It makes us stronger."

"That's easy for you to say."

"Why is it easy for me to say?"

Silas took a deep breath, inhaling the vapors of his peppermint tea. "You were born into the cold," he said. "You were raised in the mountains and they've always been a part of you. I was raised near them, but they were never mine to climb. I could always afford to look at them from afar."

"I've hiked many mountains," Vera acknowledged, "but I know you've hiked some, too. Everyone has. We all have mountains to climb."

"Yours have been taller than mine," Silas pointed out. "My mountains are hills compared to yours."

"Comparisons aside," Vera said, "they're still mountains—and you've hiked them, nonetheless."

Silas sipped his tea. "I realized something today," he said. "I was standing at the summit of the mountain that you and I climbed together when it came to me. Your grandfather helped me see it."

"What's that?"

"I can't escape the cold. I thought I could, but I can't."

"I don't know anybody who can," Vera said gently.

"What about your grandfather? He doesn't seem to mind the cold at all."

Vera half-smiled. "He may not mind it, but I wouldn't say it doesn't bother him. He runs off to the mountains every winter for a reason, you know. The cold reminds him of how my mother died."

"Still," Silas said, "in spite of everything, he manages to stay warm. You do, too." He drained his tea, then stared into the empty mug. "I don't understand how."

Vera reached over and touched his hand. Her bright blue eyes were glimmering with light. "I observe," she said.

"You observe?"

She nodded. "I learned from watching a friend of mine. He showed me how to view the world through open eyes."

"Who?" Silas said.

Vera threw a glance over her shoulder, smiling at the painting of the owl that hung above the hearth. "Him."

"Him?" Silas said. "How?"

"He showed me how to perceive," Vera said simply. "I've been watching him for years now. Owls are excellent teachers."

"Viewing the world through open eyes..." Silas said slowly. He frowned at the painting. "How is that any different from what I'm already doing? How are your eyes—and his—different than mine?"

Vera shrugged. "I'll tell you—but first, you should get some more tea."

"What?"

"First, you should get some more tea. There's no sense in moving ahead with an empty mug, is there?" She smiled. "The kettle's on the stove."

Silas got up, filled his mug, and then returned to his armchair. His ice-encased conscience had started to thaw by the time he sat back down.

"All right," Vera said. "Are you ready?"

"I'm ready."

She lowered her voice, as though afraid the owl might hear. "An owl's eyes are always open," she said.

He knitted his brow. "And mine aren't?"

"Sometimes they are," Vera said. "But other times they're very nearly shut."

"All right," Silas said. "But what about when they're open? How are they any different then?"

She patted his hand. "Even when your eyes are open, they're still bound to miss things. It's unavoidable. Owls, on the other hand, have impeccable vision. They see everything. They always have."

"Everything?"

"Everything. Even the things we miss."

"Like what?"

"The hope," she said. "The optimism. The warmth. The will to smile, even when we see that the world is cold."

Silas gazed up at the owl in the painting. "I'd like to see that. For once in my life, I'd really like to see that."

"And you can," Vera said. "There's nothing holding you back. The only thing you have to do is open your eyes."

Silas nodded, considering the mug in his grasp. For once, it was full—and that gave him hope. He smiled. When he looked up, Vera was smiling, too.

"Good," she said. "Now, keep them open. If there's one thing owls have taught me, it's that there's wisdom to be found in an all-encompassing gaze." Her blue eyes sparkled. "And where there's wisdom, there's warmth."

At that moment, Silas finally understood. "The world is cold, but the owl's truth keeps you warm..."

"Yes." Vera squeezed his hand. "And it'll keep you warm, too."

X

Silas went to bed with a smile that night. He awoke early the next morning, when the sun was peeking drowsily over the horizon. He dressed in the fleeting darkness, crept downstairs, and braced himself for the cold. Then he stepped out into the dawn, quietly closing the door behind him.

He wandered to the edge of the unplowed road, regretting the fact that he would soon be returning to Burlington. His train left today at noon. By sunset, he would be on the other side of the lake and the mountains would be a distant memory to him. He was grateful for their peace, even if he couldn't always walk among them. They had taught him more than he had ever hoped to learn.

An unmistakable chorus of hooting broke the silence of the Notch. Silas scanned the trees around him, his hushed breath rising and falling in ghostly puffs. At last, he spotted the owl. The forest and sky had swaddled it in a shroud of experience that surmounted the wit of any self-assured university man. Its breast was streaked with pale pinstripes, while the rest of its plumage took on the appearance of a sweeping frock coat. Its face was round and full and flat, and it was a wonder that its feathered spectacles didn't slip down over its beak.

The owl was eying him with interest from a low-hanging bough.

Silas grinned. *I've seen your portrait*, he thought. *I've heard your truth. It's good to finally meet you.*

The owl blinked. Its wide eyes shone with perspective. *I know*, it seemed to say. There was so much solace in so simple a phrase.

A gust of wind coursed through the Notch, and Silas shivered. *The world is cold*, he thought instinctively. He watched for his companion's reply.

The owl ruffled its tawny feathers and swiveled its gaze toward the horizon. Its eyes flashed in the soft orange light. Silas followed suit, squinting at the sunrise through the snowy trees.

Where there's wisdom, there's warmth, he thought. Vera was right.

The owl looked back at him knowingly, then turned on its perch and spread its wings. It took flight without a sound, gliding off in the direction of the sun. A flurry of feathers lingered in its wake. Silas plucked two out of the air and slipped them into his overcoat's breast pocket. They lay still against his chest, souvenirs from an early morning reverie.

He walked back to the inn and found his way to the hearth. Vera was kneeling in front of it, adding fresh logs to the dwindling flames. "You're up early," she said, smiling at him over her shoulder. "Where'd you go?"

"Nowhere far. I just stepped outside to watch the sunrise."

Vera used one of the logs to prod the ravenous fire, then stood and wiped her hands on her dress. "Even with the cold, I'm sure it was beautiful."

"It was," Silas said, "and it wasn't too cold at all."

"No?"

"Not at all. My friend kept me warm."

"What friend?"

He patted the feathers in his pocket. "Well, to be fair, he's your friend, too."

Her eyes widened. She pointed to the owl in the painting above the mantle.

Silas nodded.

"You actually saw him?"

He drew one of the feathers from his pocket and presented it to her.

She beamed, tucking it behind her ear. "Where was he?"

"Right outside, in a tree by the road."

"Really?" She sounded surprised. "He's hardly ever that close by."

"Where is he usually?"

"In the clearing by Deidre Brook. He was perched above my mother's headstone when I first found him. For weeks, that's where I set up my easel—right next to her."

Silas recalled the weathered headstone with a grimace. "I know you don't want me to feel bad, but I am sorry about what happened to her."

Vera stroked her feather absentmindedly. "So am I."

"You're damned strong, Vera. I hope you know that."

She smiled down at the feather in his breast pocket. "Thanks, Silas. It's people like you that make the world a little bit warmer."

"Of course. Not for nothing, but the gratitude goes both ways."

"Does it?"

"Absolutely. This is the warmest I've felt in years." He caught a glimpse of her easel, folded up and tucked against the wall. "Where's the painting you've been working on?"

"The view of the Notch?"

"Yes, that one."

She shrugged. "I thought I needed some distance from it, so I put it away for a while."

"Is it finished?"

She laughed. "I'm an artist. I don't know what 'finished' means."

"Fair enough," Silas said. "But all the same, I hope you plan on finishing it. It was a grand painting—one of the best you've ever done."

"I didn't know you liked it that much."

"I did—shadows and all."

"Don't look so glum," she said, rubbing his arm. "You'll see it again someday."

Silas paused. "I suppose that means I'll see you, too?"

"Only if you want to."

"Of course, I want to."

"In that case," Vera said, "if you ever find yourself back in Freedman's Notch, you'll have a place to stay." Her eyes were warm and true. "You always will."

"I'll be back," he assured her. "Trust me, I wish I didn't have to leave." He sighed. "I miss it here already."

"It'd be nice if you could stay," Vera admitted. "But you and I both know that you can't avoid the cold forever. Sooner or later, you have to step outside and face it."

"I know," Silas said. "And when I get back to Burlington, I will."

"With open eyes?"

"With open eyes," he promised.

She regarded him fondly. "Where there's wisdom, there's warmth," she said. "Remember that, won't you?"

"Always," he said.

He glanced down at the feather in his pocket and smiled. The sunrise was still playing along its silky vanes.

XI

Silas spent the rest of the morning tidying his room and organizing the contents of his rucksack. A tight bundle of clothes was the only thing he had brought along, and a small mountain of memories was the only thing he was bringing back. He made the bed, shouldered his rucksack, and took one last look around. The short stack of books on the nightstand caught his eye. He perused the titles with interest, selecting a familiar one from the middle of the stack. The book was weathered and dog-eared. Its spine was stretched and its ribbon marker was frayed. He cleared the dust from its faded red cover and ran his thumb over the angular black text.

Walden; or, Life in the Woods, it read. *By Henry David Thoreau.*

He flipped through the book with a reminiscent smile, recalling that he had first come across it at the university. He had read a chapter of it every morning back at the dimly-lit café, finishing it in a matter of weeks. Thoreau's eloquent descriptions of nature had intrigued and engrossed him, making him want to pack up his life and leave everything behind. He had never thought that he would—but now, as he held the book in his hands, he realized that he had. Way had led onto way, and he was so far from where he started.

He scanned the yellowed pages with a sigh. They reminded him of how little he liked the city, and of how much he liked it here in

Freedman's Notch. He wished that the weekend was longer, that his solace-filled sojourn didn't have to end, but nothing could change the inescapable truth.

His stay in the mountains was over. It was time for him to return to the cold.

He stared down at the book, blinking in disbelief at the words on the page. A simple declaration stood out to him amid the rambling prose. It was a statement that he himself could have written, an ode to the original owner of the feather in his breast pocket:

I rejoice that there are owls.

He smiled at the truth, closed *Walden*, and returned it to the stack of books on the nightstand. He said farewell to the room, nodded at the owl carving on the door, and descended the uneven staircase.

Vera was waiting for him on the landing, her owl feather still tucked behind her ear. "Ready?"

"As I'll ever be."

They set out half an hour before noon, bound for the train station at the entrance of the Notch. The winding road led them away from the hulking mountains and across a snowy plain. Time and time again, Silas found himself looking back at the way they came, trying to sear the sweeping valley into his rueful mind.

The station was just as lonely as it was the day he had arrived. The accompanying offices were still dark, and there were no porters in sight. Silas checked his watch. The train was minutes away. He and Vera stood on the platform, huddled together against the cold.

"Hopefully, it'll be warmer the next time I see you," she said.

"Don't worry," he said. "I'll be back in the spring."

Vera made a face. "Don't come back in the spring. There's rain and mud—blackflies, too."

Silas laughed. "All right, then. What about in the summer?"

"You'll love it here in the summer. The mountains are beautiful then. They're beautiful now, but..." She grinned. The sunlight was dancing in her eyes.

"I know what you mean."

"The wind will be warmer," she continued. "The trees will be greener, and the snow will be all but gone. You'll have finished your term at the university, and my grandfather will be back running the inn. There'll be so much more time to explore, so many more summits to see..."

"I long for warmer days," Silas said. "Sometimes it feels like winter will never end."

"It will, eventually," Vera assured him. "And when it does, the mountains will be waiting." She squeezed his hand. "I'll be waiting, too."

The train pulled into the station with a strident blast of its whistle.

Silas sighed. "The waiting begins..."

Vera hugged him. He winced as the cold nipped at his face. "Thank you," he whispered.

She drew back, brushing the hair out of her eyes. "For what?"

"For giving me hope," he said. "For keeping me warm, and for opening my eyes..."

"Always." She hugged him once more. When they separated, she patted the owl feather tucked in the pocket against his heart. "I'll see you soon."

Silas nodded. "Yes, you will."

He crossed the barren platform and climbed aboard the train. An attendant welcomed him onto the car and checked his ticket. All of the seats were empty.

He sat by the window and waved to Vera on the platform until the train shrieked and rattled away. At length, the station disappeared and Freedman's Notch faded from view. The mountains were all that remained, white with wisdom in the distance.

Silas settled into his seat, not bothering to take off his rucksack, and frowned. Something hard and rectangular was pressing into his back.

He immediately dumped the contents of his rucksack onto his lap. As he rummaged through them, he realized that his clothes had been painstakingly swaddled around a very thin box. He unwrapped the bundle and broke into a grin. An all-too-familiar view of Freedman's Notch was spread out on the canvas before him. The artist had left her initials on the bottom righthand corner of the painting:

V.B.

Silas admired her masterpiece, running his hand over her countless careful brushstrokes. The Notch's sloping headwalls were stark and shadowed; sunlit and stunning. A log cabin, though new to the painting, occupied its longstanding place in the foreground. There was smoke streaming from its stout chimney and candles glowing in its miniscule windows. A wandering series of snowshoe tracks led up to its wide-open door.

He turned the painting over in his hands and saw, with a start, that Vera had left him a message. It was a single sentence, written in simple black cursive:

The world is cold, but always remember: where there is wisdom, there is warmth.

Silas shifted his gaze to the owl feather in his pocket, then raised his eyes to the window. He smiled at the mountains on the horizon, seeing for himself that Vera's words rang true.

—~—~—~—~—

THE WORLD IS COLD,
BUT ALWAYS REMEMBER:

WHERE THERE IS WISDOM,
THERE IS WARMTH.

—~—~—~—~—

Michael Lajoie is an avid oceanside explorer, mountain climber, and wilderness lover. His debut novella, *The Summit by the Sea*, was published in 2020. He lives in Seacoast New Hampshire with his family.

CPSIA information can be obtained
at www.ICGtesting.com
Printed in the USA
BVHW040358290921
617592BV00007B/11